"I'm going to go through the haunted house first thing," Charlie Cashman bragged to Jessica. "Maybe I'll see the goblin everyone's talking about."

"I'm going to go there last," Jessica said as she got on the bus behind him. "The rides and booths are going to be more fun."

Charlie turned and rolled his eyes. "I bet you're too chicken to go in the haunted house. You *are* a girl."

Jessica stuck her tongue out at Charlie.

"Don't let him bother you," Elizabeth whispered in Jessica's ear. She followed Jessica to the back of the bus.

"I don't care what Charlie says," Jessica said, plopping down in a seat by the window. "I just wish he would leave me alone."

Bantam Skylark Books in the SWEET VALLEY KIDS series

SWEET VALLEY KIDS

JESSICA GETS SPOOKED

Written by
Molly Mia Stewart

Created by
FRANCINE PASCAL

Illustrated by
Ying-Hwa Hu

A BANTAM SKYLARK BOOK ®
NEW YORK · TORONTO · LONDON · SYDNEY · AUCKLAND

RL 2, 005-008

JESSICA GETS SPOOKED

A Bantam Skylark Book / October 1993

*Sweet Valley High® and Sweet Valley Kids are
trademarks of Francine Pascal*

Conceived by Francine Pascal

*Produced by Daniel Weiss Associates, Inc.
33 West 17th Street
New York, NY 10011*

Cover art by Susan Tang

*Skylark Books is a registered trademark of Bantam Books, a
division of Bantam Doubleday Dell Publishing Group, Inc.
Registered in U.S. Patent and Trademark Office and elsewhere.*

*All rights reserved.
Copyright © 1993 by Francine Pascal.
Cover art and interior illustrations copyright © 1993 by
Daniel Weiss Associates, Inc.
No part of this book may be reproduced or transmitted
in any form or by any means, electronic or mechanical,
including photocopying, recording, or by any information
storage and retrieval system, without permission in
writing from the publisher.
For information address: Bantam Books.*

---

*If you purchased this book without a cover you should be aware
that this book is stolen property. It was reported as "unsold and
destroyed" to the publisher and neither the author nor the
publisher has received any payment for this "stripped book."*

ISBN: 0-553-48094-4

Published simultaneously in the United States and Canada

Bantam Books are published by Bantam Books, a division of Bantam
Doubleday Dell Publishing Group, Inc. Its trademark, consisting of the
words "Bantam Books" and the portrayal of a rooster, is Registered in
U.S. Patent and Trademark Office and in other countries. Marca
Registrada. Bantam Books, 1540 Broadway, New York, New York 10036.

PRINTED IN THE UNITED STATES OF AMERICA

CWO   0 9 8 7 6 5 4 3 2 1

CHAPTER 1

A Spooky Rumor

"Do you think it's true?" Elizabeth Wakefield asked.

Her twin sister, Jessica, shook her head so hard that her ponytail swung back and forth. "No. It's only a dumb rumor."

"Well, I kind of hope not," Elizabeth said as they headed toward Sweet Valley Elementary School's parking lot one morning. "It would be great if the haunted house at Enchanted Forest really *was* haunted."

The twins' second-grade class was spending the day at Enchanted Forest, one of the largest amusement parks in California. The trip had been planned as a pre-Halloween treat.

"You can always pretend it's haunted," Jessica said.

Elizabeth knew she could. She had a vivid imagination. She loved reading books and daydreaming about magic spells and trips to faraway lands. Elizabeth also loved sports and was proud to be a member of the Sweet Valley Soccer League. Jessica was different. Instead of reading, she enjoyed playing dress-up and going to modern-dance class. Messy sports weren't for her. She preferred indoor games so that her clothes wouldn't get dirty.

But even though they enjoyed different things, Jessica and Elizabeth had a lot in common. For one thing, they looked exactly alike. That's because they weren't just twins—they were *identical* twins!

Both girls had blue-green eyes and long blond hair with bangs. They shared a bedroom and toys and chores. Elizabeth and Jessica both loved being twins. It was like having a built-in best friend.

"But everyone's heard about the goblin in the haunted house," Elizabeth said. "He's supposed to have hair growing on his teeth, and big yellow eyes that pop out of his head."

"Oh, come on, Liz," Jessica said. "There's no such thing as a goblin. Or any kind of monster. You told me so when I was having bad dreams, remember?"

Elizabeth frowned. "I know, but . . ."

"Jessica, Elizabeth," someone called, waving them over. It was Lila Fowler. She was Jessica's best friend after Elizabeth, and she was standing in front of the bus that was taking the class to Enchanted Forest. Many of their other classmates were already there too.

"You finally got here," Lila said. She readjusted the headband in her light-brown hair. "I thought we'd have to leave without you."

"It's still early," Jessica said. "The bus doors aren't even open."

"My dad drove me to school so I wouldn't be late," Ellen Riteman said.

"I was so excited, I couldn't sleep last night."

"Me neither," Elizabeth said. "I kept thinking about the Halloween goblin."

"I heard he attacks someone every year before Halloween," Eva Simpson said. She had moved to Sweet Valley a while ago from Jamaica, an island in the Caribbean, and she loved American holidays. "Halloween is just three days away."

Jessica shook her head. "Those rumors are silly. There's no goblin."

"It *is* so real," Lila said. "Everyone knows about Billy Cooper. He went inside the haunted house on his second-grade trip two years ago—and never came out."

"I thought the Coopers moved away," Jessica said.

"They did," Lila confirmed. "Because they were so sad about what happened to Billy."

Elizabeth shivered. "See, Jess."

"I guess we'd better be careful," Eva said.

"Are you talking about the goblin?" Todd Wilkins asked as he and Kisho Murasaki joined them.

"Yes," Elizabeth answered.

Kisho whispered something in Todd's ear. Both of them cracked up.

"What's so funny?" Elizabeth asked.

Kisho and Todd exchanged looks.

"You wouldn't understand," Kisho said.

"Why not?" Elizabeth wanted to know.

The boys looked nervous. "Because you're a girl," Todd finally said.

Elizabeth knew that wasn't the *real* reason. Todd and Kisho played with her all the time. Todd was even on the soccer league with her, and they always had fun together. Elizabeth decided to ignore them. And anyway, the bus driver had just opened the bus doors. Everyone began to climb aboard.

"I'm going to go through the haunted house first thing," Elizabeth heard Charlie Cashman brag to Jessica. Charlie was one of the biggest boys in the second grade. He could be a bully, and lately he had been picking on Jessica.

"I'm going to go there last," Jessica said as she got on the bus behind him. "The rides and booths are going to be more fun."

Charlie turned and rolled his eyes. "I bet you're too chicken to go in the haunted house. You *are* a girl."

Jessica stuck her tongue out at Charlie.

"Don't let him bother you," Elizabeth whispered in her sister's ear. She followed Jessica to the back of the bus.

"I don't care what Charlie says," Jessica said, plopping down in a seat by the window. "I just wish he would leave me alone."

CHAPTER 2

Green Slime

"Sixteen, eighteen . . ." Mrs. Otis, the twins' teacher, was counting as she stood at the front of the bus. When she got to twenty-two, she turned to the driver. "OK, everyone's here. Time to go!"

"Hurray! Hurray!" Winston Egbert yelled out as the bus took off. He was the class clown. All of the other kids cheered.

"We're on our way," Elizabeth said to Jessica with a big smile.

Jessica nodded and was about to say something when her head was jerked back. Charlie was sitting in the seat directly behind. He had pulled on Jessica's ponytail.

"Cut it out," Jessica said, spinning around to face him.

"You want me to stop?" Charlie asked.

"Yes," Jessica said. She turned and faced forward again.

"Are you sure?" Charlie asked.

"Yes!" Jessica said, not bothering to look at him.

"OK, I won't pull your hair anymore," Charlie promised.

"He better not," Jessica muttered to Elizabeth.

"Forget Charlie," Eva said. She and Amy Sutton were sitting next to the

11

twins, on the other side of the aisle. She leaned across. "I heard the Halloween goblin bites off people's toes," Eva said.

"Why would he do that?" Jessica asked.

"To make toe soup," Eva said.

Elizabeth giggled.

"I heard that one look from the Halloween goblin can make your hair stand on end forever!" Amy said.

"I don't know," Jessica said, shaking her head. "All these rumors—"

"Maybe *that's* what happened to Winston!" Elizabeth interrupted.

Jessica laughed.

"Hey, who's making fun of my hair?" Winston shouted from the rear. His hair was short and bristly. "I've never seen the goblin."

"Just a bad barber," Todd joked.

Jessica laughed some more. Then she reached back and touched her ponytail. She felt something cold and gooey.

"Lizzie?" Jessica whispered. "What's on my hair?"

Elizabeth turned to look. Jessica saw her make a face. "It's—it's slime," Elizabeth said.

"Eww," Jessica screamed, jumping up from her seat. "Mrs. Otis, help!"

She turned and glared at Charlie. "You did this," she said accusingly. The whole class knew that Charlie was going to be the Monster from the Green Lagoon on Halloween. He had been talking about it for weeks.

"Me?" Charlie said, trying to sound innocent.

13

"Yes, you, Charlie Cashman," Jessica said. "I hate you!"

"Quiet down," Mrs. Otis said as she walked down the aisle. She took one look at Jessica's hair and sighed. "That's not going to be easy to get off," she said. "Jessica, come up front with me and I'll see what I can do. Charlie, we're going to have to talk about this when we get back to school. Until then, I want you to stay away from Jessica."

"All right," Charlie muttered.

Jerry McAllister, who was sitting with Charlie, laughed. Charlie punched Jerry in the arm.

Jessica glared at them both before walking to the front of the bus. She let Mrs. Otis take her hair down and tried to sit still while the teacher combed the

14

slime out into tissues. It took a long time.

She could hear her friends laughing in the back of the bus. She was missing all of the fun. The only good thing was that Charlie couldn't bother her.

"I think I'm finished," Mrs. Otis said finally, combing Jessica's hair back into a ponytail. "And guess where we are?"

Jessica looked out the window. The bus was heading up a winding road. As they rounded a bend, Jessica could see a colorful sign that said WELCOME TO ENCHANTED FOREST.

"We're here!" Jessica called out.

Everyone began talking at once as the bus drove through the gates of the amusement park and headed to the nearby parking lot. Jessica ran back to her seat. Mrs. Otis stood up and raised a hand for silence. It took a few minutes for everyone to settle down.

"I have an admission pass, plus a packet of tickets for each of you," Mrs. Otis announced. "You can go wherever you like as long as you stick with the partner you chose last week."

The twins exchanged smiles. Jessica was Elizabeth's partner, and Elizabeth was Jessica's partner.

"Drop your bagged lunches in this cardboard box as you get off the bus," Mrs. Otis went on. "We'll meet at the picnic area at twelve o'clock sharp to eat."

Elizabeth and Jessica nodded solemnly.

"Now, where are we going to meet?" Mrs. Otis asked.

"At the picnic area!" everyone shouted at once.

"OK. Now get out of here and have fun!" Mrs. Otis said.

One at a time, the kids jumped off the bus.

"Hurry," Jessica called to Elizabeth as she started to run.

CHAPTER 3

A Stickup

"Welcome to Enchanted Forest," said a young woman wearing a cat suit.

"Thanks." Elizabeth handed the woman her admission pass and got a sticker in exchange. The sticker showed a witch flying on a broomstick.

"It glows in the dark," the woman said. "And a moon appears in the background."

"Neat." Elizabeth stuck it to her

T-shirt. "I'll put it on my pajamas tonight."

"So will I," Jessica said as a man dressed as a werewolf took her pass and handed her a sticker. "Happy Halloween!"

"Hurry up," Todd said from behind them. He was next in line.

Elizabeth and Jessica each pushed through the turnstile, then walked into a glass tunnel. When they came out on the other side, they were on Main Street in Enchanted Forest.

A beautiful fountain with mermaid and dolphin sculptures stood at the center of the street. Water splashed down from way up high.

"Wow!" Elizabeth said.

Jessica nodded. "I love it already."

"I see the roller coaster," Amy yelled.

"And there's the Ferris wheel," Lila said, pointing in the distance.

Ellen jumped up and down in excitement.

"Where should we go first?" Kisho asked.

"How about the haunted house?" Eva suggested.

"No," Todd said. "It's not ready yet."

"What do you mean?" Elizabeth asked.

"I mean—*I'm* not ready for the haunted house yet," Todd said quickly. "Let's ride the Super Coaster. That's my all-time favorite."

"I want to try the bumper cars," Eva said.

"Bumper cars?" Ellen said. "Cool!"

Jessica hugged herself. "This is

great. There's so much to do."

"You can start by putting your hands up," came a loud voice.

Everyone spun around.

"Reach for the sky!"

It was Charlie. He was standing next to a Wild West shop with his hands on his hips. Jerry was with him.

"Why don't you go away?" Jessica muttered.

"What did you say?" Charlie asked.

"I said, why don't you go away!" Jessica yelled. "Go jump in a lake."

"Nobody talks to me like that," Charlie said. In a flash, he pulled a water gun out of his jeans pocket and squirted Jessica right in the face.

"You stupid creep," Jessica shouted, wiping the water off.

21

Jerry grinned. "Charlie told you to put 'em up." He followed Charlie down Main Street.

"Hey!" Todd called after them. "Where are you going?"

"I've got stuff to do," Charlie said. "You know what I mean?"

"Wait for us." Todd pulled on Kisho's arm. "Come on. Let's go."

"You're going with Charlie and Jerry?" Elizabeth asked. She knew Kisho was good friends with Charlie, but he and Todd had said they would do things with her and Jessica that day.

"Yes," Kisho said. "But you can't come."

Elizabeth was puzzled. "How come you guys are acting so mysterious?"

"None of your business, Elizabeth

Wakefield," Charlie yelled out.

Kisho and Todd ran after him.

"See you later, Elizabeth," Todd called back.

Elizabeth shook her head. She felt disappointed that Todd and Kisho weren't going to spend the day with her. She didn't understand why they were purposely leaving her out.

"Let's go to King Abelard's Castle first," Jessica suggested. "It's just over there."

"OK," Elizabeth agreed.

Jessica took Elizabeth's hand and started toward the castle. "Come on," she called to Lila, Ellen, Amy, and Eva. "We have to hurry."

But the other girls didn't follow.

"Aren't you coming?" Jessica asked.

"No," Lila said. "Charlie's always hanging around you lately. I don't want to be near him. He's disgusting."

"Don't blame me," Jessica said angrily. "I didn't invite him."

"Ellen and I are going on the Super Coaster first," Lila said.

"What about you?" Elizabeth asked Amy and Eva.

Amy looked down. "I think we'll try the roller coaster too. See you later."

"Fine," Jessica said, stomping away.

Elizabeth followed. She had a strange feeling that something big was going to happen that day.

CHAPTER 4

A Soggy Ride

King Abelard's Castle was a huge, gray stone building with tall towers. It looked like something out of a fairy tale. A moat separated the castle from the rest of the park. Tall trees surrounded it, making it look enchanted.

Elizabeth and Jessica quickly got in line. A man in a jester's outfit collected tickets and helped each of them put on a life jacket. Then it was time to board a wooden boat that floated to the castle through the dark water. Elizabeth leaned over.

"Liz, look out!" Jessica yelled.

An alligator suddenly appeared from behind one of the rocks. He swam straight toward the boat and snapped his giant teeth at Elizabeth. She jumped back and bumped against Jessica.

"That was close," Elizabeth said, shaking.

"It's just a fake," Jessica said. "But still scary."

Elizabeth laughed. "I know. And look over there." She pointed to a tree on shore. "There's a huge snake on the top branch."

"Yuck!" Jessica scrunched up her nose. She didn't like snakes.

The boat floated around another rock

and glided into the castle. To the right was a courtyard filled with people belonging to the king's court. A magician stood waving his wand over a kettle of magical brew. Ladies in high pointed hats clapped as a court jester did flips while juggling flaming sticks in the air.

It was magical—until the twins were hit by a big splash of water and the spell was broken. Jessica turned around and saw Charlie and Jerry in the boat behind them. Charlie was grinning.

"Cut it out," Jessica told him.

"Yeah, go pick on someone else," Elizabeth shouted.

Charlie laughed and splashed them some more. He splashed them as they floated by King Abelard feasting on roasted pig. He splashed them as they passed by two knights fighting on horseback. He splashed them as their boat floated out of the castle, into the sunlight, and back to the start of the ride.

"No splashing, please," one of the attendants yelled at Charlie. Charlie finally stopped. But by then, Jessica and Elizabeth were soaked.

"What happened?" Charlie innocently asked the twins as they all climbed out of their boats. "You two are all wet."

"Did you fall out of your boat or something?" Jerry asked, laughing.

Elizabeth sighed. "Very funny. And where did you come from, anyway? There was no one behind us in line."

"I guess we just crept up on you," Charlie said.

"And if you're not careful, maybe we'll

creep up on you again," Jerry added.

"You—"

"Don't waste your breath," Jessica interrupted Elizabeth. "Just ignore them the way we ignore Steven when he bothers us," she said, whispering in Elizabeth's ear. Steven was their older brother. He loved to tease them.

"See you guys later," Charlie said at the end of the path. "It's been fun."

The twins watched Charlie and Jerry walk toward the shooting galleries.

"What do you want to do now?" Elizabeth asked Jessica.

Jessica looked down at her wet sweatshirt. "Push Charlie into the ocean."

Elizabeth giggled.

Winston and Andy Franklin ran up to them.

"Were you on the water slide?" Winston asked.

"No," Elizabeth said. "King Abelard's Castle."

"I didn't know that was a water ride," Winston said, looking at them from head to toe.

Jessica sighed. "It's not."

"Have you tried the haunted house yet?" Andy asked.

"No," Jessica said.

"We just did," Winston said. "It's great."

"Did you see the goblin?" Elizabeth asked.

"*We* didn't," Winston said, with a knowing look. "But maybe he's waiting for *you*!"

CHAPTER 5

Trapped

"Let's go to the haunted house right now," Jessica said. "I don't want to save it for last anymore."

Elizabeth watched as Winston and Andy ran toward a cotton-candy stand. She was frowning. "I think Winston and Andy have a secret," Elizabeth said. "And it might be the same one Todd and Kisho are hiding."

"So?" Jessica asked.

"So, I don't know," Elizabeth said.

"But I think we should try the bumper cars."

"We could go to the haunted house and then come back," Jessica suggested.

"But the bumper cars are right here," Elizabeth said. "Sort of."

She grabbed Jessica's hand and dragged her past several rides until they got to the bumper cars. She hoped Jessica would forget about the haunted house if they did something else. Elizabeth was determined not to go near the haunted house until she found out what the boys were up to.

"You'll be good at this," Elizabeth encouraged Jessica. "Remember the derby?"

"Definitely!" Jessica had won first prize in the Sweet Valley Elementary School Soap Box Derby. She had driven a car Elizabeth had built. "Come on. I'm going to do some major bumping."

Elizabeth hid a smile. Jessica had changed her mind awfully fast.

While they waited in line, they watched kids drive cars with huge rubber bumpers. Most of the cars were green or blue, but there was one red one. The kids made their cars go as fast as possible and then headed them right into their friends' cars. When the cars crashed together, they bounced off of one another. Everyone was laughing.

"I want the red one," Jessica told Elizabeth.

When the attendant opened up the

gate, Jessica ran straight to the red car. Elizabeth ran to a green one. As she put her seat belt on, Elizabeth saw Charlie and Jerry run in. Charlie slid into the only car left. It was right next to Jessica's.

"Look out, Jess," Elizabeth warned her.

Jessica nodded. She pretended not to see Charlie, but she couldn't ignore him for long. As soon as the ride started, Charlie bumped her.

Jessica hit the gas pedal, turned her steering wheel hard, and bumped Charlie back. Charlie was knocked sideways in his seat. That made Jessica laugh.

But Charlie looked angry. He turned his car and bumped Jessica *really* hard. Then he drove just far enough away to

pick up speed to bump her again. Charlie hit Jessica's car over and over.

Jessica tried to bump Charlie back, but he was faster than she was. He pushed her car into a corner. Jessica couldn't get out by turning left because a wall was in her way. She couldn't get out by turning right because Charlie was there. Jessica was trapped.

From across the rink, Elizabeth saw Jessica fold her arms across her chest. Her sister wasn't even trying to fight back anymore.

Elizabeth frowned. She had to help Jessica get away. Quickly she drove her car over and bumped Charlie hard from behind. "Stop following us," she shouted at him. "Don't you have anything better to do?"

CHAPTER 6

A Close Call

As Jessica and Elizabeth walked away from the bumper cars, Jessica still had her arms crossed. "Charlie makes me so mad," she said.

"Me, too," Elizabeth said. "He thinks he's funny. But he's not. He's just ruining our fun."

"At least he's not around now," Jessica said. Charlie and Jerry had disappeared as soon as the ride had ended.

"Yeah," Elizabeth said. "But I have a feeling he'll be back soon."

They turned down Main Street. Jessica ran ahead to peer into a shop window where hundreds of tiny glass animals were displayed.

Elizabeth hurried to catch up. "Look at the horse," she said, nearly out of breath. "Isn't it beautiful?"

Jessica wrinkled her nose. "I don't like horses. I think the unicorn is prettier."

"Horses and unicorns are almost the same," Elizabeth said.

Jessica shook her head. "No, they're not. Horses are big and smelly. Unicorns are magical."

Elizabeth laughed. "I still like the horse."

They went from shop to shop, looking in all the windows. Soon they came to a store that was painted in bright rainbow colors.

"Let's go inside," Elizabeth suggested.

Jessica nodded. "I want to buy a souvenir. I bet this would be a good place."

A string of bells above the door jingled as they walked in. Jessica could see spyglasses, cap guns, and a big bottle that was labeled (DISAPPEARING) INK.

"This place is full of great stuff," Elizabeth said, looking all around her.

"Look, itching powder," Jessica said. She went to one of the countertops. "Robin would like this." Robin was the twins' cousin. She liked to play jokes. Robin had visited the Wakefields a while ago and the girls had pulled lots of pranks on Steven.

"Wait," Elizabeth said. She turned

41

her back to Jessica. Then she turned around again, wearing a pig nose.

Jessica giggled. "That would be great for Halloween."

"You mean great as part of a costume for Steven," Elizabeth said. Steven was famous for his appetite.

Elizabeth wandered to the back of the store to look at comic books.

Jessica walked over to a shelf. It held jars of plastic bugs, rubber warts, trick glasses, and other neat stuff. Jessica was examining a magic wand when she saw Charlie come in. Jerry, Kisho, and Todd were with him. Quickly Jessica walked back to where Elizabeth was flipping through a Batman comic.

"The pest is here," Jessica whispered. "Let's go."

Elizabeth looked up just in time to see Charlie pick up a huge rock and throw it at her and Jessica.

"Duck!" Elizabeth yelled, pulling Jessica down on the floor.

The rock landed right where they had been standing—and bounced. It was made out of foam rubber.

The boys laughed and laughed. Jerry held his sides. Charlie had tears in his eyes.

"I hope we get to laugh at *them* soon," Elizabeth whispered to Jessica.

Together they brushed themselves off and walked past Charlie, Kisho, Todd, and Jerry without even looking at them.

"Boys are so stupid," Jessica said loudly as they stepped out the door.

CHAPTER 7

Boy Secrets

*B*ong, *bong, bong, bong, bong* . . .
"Hey, what time is it?" Jessica asked.

Elizabeth looked up at the big clock tower. "It's noon."

"Oops," Jessica said.

"We're supposed to meet Mrs. Otis," they said at exactly the same time. They joined hands and started off toward the picnic area.

"What do you think will happen if we're late?" Jessica asked as they ran.

"Maybe we'll turn into pumpkins," Elizabeth said. "That's what happened to Cinderella's carriage."

"Or maybe we'll be Halloween jack-o-lanterns," Jessica said, smiling. When the twins got to the picnic area, they took their lunches out of the big box Mrs. Otis had been watching. Then they sat down next to their friends.

"Are you having a good time?" Elizabeth asked.

"Of course," Lila said. "We went on the Super Coaster, the Ferris wheel, the water slide—"

"I won this elephant at one of the booths," Ellen said, interrupting Lila. She held up a large, purple stuffed elelphant.

"And we didn't see Charlie all morning," Lila added.

Jessica frowned. "Elizabeth and I are having fun too."

"But you *did* see Charlie," Lila said. "We heard about it."

Jessica didn't say anything. She just took a huge bite of her tuna-fish sandwich. She glared at Lila as she chewed.

Elizabeth knew her sister would never complain about Charlie in front of Lila. Lila was too much of an I-told-you-so person, and Jessica would never in a million years want to admit that Charlie was driving her crazy.

"Eva and I went through the haunted house five times," Amy said. "It's great!"

"Full of spooky surprises. I was really scared," Eva said. She took a sip of her juice. "The skeleton was the best. At first it glowed all green, then it fell in a bubbling pot of something and came out all red. Only its teeth stayed bright gold and kept chattering."

"And you never saw the goblin?" Elizabeth asked with a shiver.

Amy shrugged. "I guess *nobody* has yet. Everyone's been through at least once now."

"We haven't," Jessica said.

The other girls exchanged surprised looks.

"What are you waiting for?" Lila asked.

"Are you afraid?" Ellen said. "Just like Charlie said?"

Jessica shook her head. "Of course not. We're going as soon as lunch ends. Right, Elizabeth?"

48

Elizabeth didn't answer. She got up and went over to Kisho. He was just sitting down to eat his lunch.

"Charlie has been acting like a creep all day," Elizabeth complained.

"I guess," Kisho said, with a shrug. "He says Jessica can't take a joke."

"She can too!" Elizabeth said. "And anyway, what does that have to do with Charlie?"

"He's going to teach her how," Kisho said simply.

Elizabeth shook her head. "I wish Charlie would mind his own beeswax."

Todd came over with his lunch bag and poked Kisho in the arm. "What are you talking to Elizabeth for?" he whispered.

Elizabeth heard what Todd said. She

noticed that he sounded alarmed.

"Don't worry," Kisho said. "I didn't tell her."

"Tell me *what*?" Elizabeth demanded.

Todd and Kisho exchanged looks.

"Nothing," Kisho said.

"A secret," Todd said at the same time.

Elizabeth crossed her arms. "Tell me what's going on—or else," she ordered.

"We can't," Kisho said. "It's a secret. A secret for boys. No girls can know, or else it'll be ruined."

"Charlie says girls can't keep secrets," Todd added.

"That's stupid," Elizabeth said. "You guys have told me lots of secrets. I've always kept my lips tight as a zipper."

Todd and Kisho looked at each other.

"Remember what happened at soccer practice last week?" Elizabeth asked Todd.

Todd looked up fast. "Nobody knows about that!" He dropped his voice to a whisper. "Even Kisho."

Elizabeth smiled. "That's right. Nobody knows because I didn't tell anyone." She looked at Kisho. "And remember what you told me about your grade on last week's spelling test?"

Kisho turned red. "You promised not to tell."

"I know," Elizabeth said. "And I haven't. I'm good at keeping secrets."

"I guess," Todd said. "But this secret has to do with Jessica. Do you still promise not to tell?"

Elizabeth wasn't surprised. "Promise," she said.

"Cross your heart?" Kisho asked.

"Cross my heart," Elizabeth said. "Hope to die. Stick a needle in my eye."

Kisho looked at Todd. They still seemed uncertain.

"Spit," Todd said.

Elizabeth sighed. "Come on, Todd."

"Spit," Todd repeated.

"Oh, all right," Elizabeth said. She spat into her hand. Todd spat into his hand. They shook.

"OK, will you tell me what the big secret is *now*?" Elizabeth asked.

Todd nodded at Kisho.

Kisho started whispering in Elizabeth's ear. By the time he finished, Elizabeth was frowning.

CHAPTER 8

Splat!

Jessica rolled up her lunch bag and threw it in the garbage. "Can we go now?"

"As soon as I finish," Elizabeth said.

Most of their friends had already left the picnic area. Even Mrs. Otis had gone. But Elizabeth was taking forever to eat the last of her carrot sticks. She was making Jessica feel impatient. Very impatient.

"Come on," Jessica said. "I want to go to the haunted house."

"Look!" Elizabeth exclaimed. "Ice cream!" She got up and skipped toward a booth on the edge of the picnic area. Its roof looked like an enormous ice-cream cone turned upside down.

"I'd like a chocolate cone," Elizabeth told the man in the booth.

Jessica was happy. Elizabeth had finally finished her bagged lunch. Dessert couldn't take long. "I want a swirl," Jessica said.

"Don't the identical twins want identical ice-cream cones?" the man asked.

"No!" Elizabeth and Jessica said together.

The ice-cream man smiled. "All right, then. One chocolate and one swirl coming right up." He pulled down a lever on a big silver machine and filled one cone with chocolate ice cream. He handed that one to Elizabeth. Then he pulled two levers down halfway and made a perfect swirl for Jessica.

Jessica handed the man some money and took her cone. "This is delicious," she said, swallowing her first lick.

"Yummy," Elizabeth agreed with a big smile.

Jessica took another lick. But just then Charlie ran up behind her and gave her a shove. Jessica dropped her cone.

"Oops!" Charlie said, grinning. "Sorry."

Jessica looked down at her ice cream. It was splattered all over the ground. "I hate you!" she shouted at Charlie.

"I hate you," Charlie mimicked Jessica.

Jessica was near tears. Charlie's non-stop jokes and pranks were spoiling her entire day at Enchanted Forest. She didn't understand why he was picking on her—and only her.

"Charlie!" Jerry appeared around the corner. "We're waiting for you. It's time."

"I'll share with you," Elizabeth told Jessica after Charlie had gone.

Jessica forced herself to smile. "Thanks."

They sat down on a bench to finish the ice cream. A teenage boy and girl walked by, holding hands and laughing. They kissed on the lips.

"Gross!" Elizabeth and Jessica both said.

The teenagers stopped to buy drinks

at a stand. Then they began walking across the picnic lawn. Elizabeth and Jessica watched as the boy took an ice cube from his paper cup and put it down the back of the girl's shirt. The girl shrieked, then laughed.

Jessica shook her head. "Is that how a boy acts when he likes a girl? Boys are so stupid."

CHAPTER 9

Last Chance

"Ok—get ready—Geronimo!" Jessica yelled.

She and Elizabeth were at the top of a huge slide. They had climbed up a ladder to get there. Now they each flopped down on felt mats they had carried up. The long slide snaked below them. The ground looked far away.

Jessica pushed off first.

Elizabeth was right behind her.

The wind blew Jessica's hair back.

"Woo-ooo," Elizabeth screamed as

she flew down the slide. Suddenly she was at the bottom. It seemed as if the ride had only taken a few seconds, but she was breathless.

"That was fun!" Jessica said. She helped her sister pick up their mats and threw them back on a huge pile next to the slide.

"What do you want to do now?" Elizabeth asked.

Jessica thought for a second. "We've been on the water ride and the moon-walk—"

"And the Mirror Maze," Elizabeth interrupted.

Jessica nodded. "We went on the Ferris wheel."

"And the Super Coaster," Elizabeth said. "Twice."

"Don't forget the merry-go-round," Jessica said. "I wouldn't do that again, though. It's for babies."

"But the Ape Man's Safari ride was fun," Elizabeth added.

"And so was Ali Baba's Treasure Hunt," Jessica said.

Elizabeth laughed. "I don't think there's anything left."

"Yes, there is," Jessica said. "The haunted house! I've been waiting to go there since lunch."

Suddenly Elizabeth's smile disappeared. "Not yet."

"Look!" Jessica pointed. "I can see it. It's right around the corner."

"Let's go later," Elizabeth said.

"It *is* later," Jessica said. She started walking toward the haunted house.

Elizabeth didn't move. "Wait!" she called.

Jessica turned around and put her hands on her hips. "This is our last chance, Elizabeth. It's almost time to go home."

Elizabeth hurried to catch up. She glanced over her shoulder. "I wonder where Charlie is," she said. "He's been following us all day. Now it's like he disappeared."

"Good!" Jessica said. "He can drop off the earth for all I care."

"But you don't have any tickets left. You used them all up at the shooting range."

"You still have a bunch left," Jessica pointed out.

"I want to save them," Elizabeth said.

"What for?" Jessica sighed. "You were really excited about going to the haunted house this morning. If we don't go now we never will."

With each step they were getting near to the haunted house. Elizabeth slowed down. "I don't know . . ."

"Well, I'm going," Jessica said. She snatched a ticket out of Elizabeth's hand. "You can stay here by yourself if you want to."

"What about the goblin?" Elizabeth asked.

"What about it?" Jessica frowned. "I'm not afraid of that silly Halloween goblin. Since when are you?"

Elizabeth was out of excuses. She knew she couldn't stop Jessica from going into the haunted house. And she couldn't warn Jessica, either. If only she hadn't promised Kisho and Todd she wouldn't tell.

Elizabeth sighed. "I'd better go with you."

CHAPTER 10

The Goblin

Holding hands, Jessica and Elizabeth walked up to the haunted house. A tall figure dressed in a hooded black cape was guarding the door. His eyes were two glowing green circles. He opened the door with an eerie creak.

"Enter if you dare!" the hooded figure croaked.

Elizabeth dragged her feet, but Jessica pulled her inside.

They tiptoed down a dim hallway full of shadows. Cobwebs hung from the ceiling. Bats cried out as they flew over-head. Then everything was quiet.

"Ahhh!" Elizabeth screamed sud-denly.

A witch flew down on them, laughing an evil laugh. Her broomstick brushed the tops of the twins' heads.

"We have guests," the witch cackled. "Welcome! Ha! Ha! Ha!"

A door at the end of the hallway swung open all by itself. Elizabeth and Jessica inched through. Inside the small room they saw a black coffin on a plat-form. A soft humming noise started just as the door behind them slammed shut.

Jessica's eyes were wide. "How do we get out?" she asked.

A door on the other side of the room opened slowly.

"Over there," Elizabeth whispered. "We have to go past the coffin first."

Carefully they tiptoed across the room. Jessica was becoming nervous. Everything was quiet again—too quiet to feel safe. Then she saw the coffin lid start to open. At the same time, someone tapped her on the shoulder. Jessica jumped. She spun around. So did Elizabeth. They both gasped.

Right in front of them was the most horrible-looking creature they had ever seen. His face was covered in green slime, and he had yellow eyes that bulged out of his head.

"I am the Halloween goblin," the creature said, opening his mouth wide to reveal sharp teeth. He pointed to Jessica. "And you are my victim! I am going to cut off your hair and toes for my soup!"

Jessica gasped. She reached for Elizabeth's hand.

The goblin drew himself up taller. "First I am going to hang you upside down until your face turns purple." He stuck his terrifying face close to Jessica's. "It's a special treat to be chosen by the Halloween goblin," he added, laughing nastily.

The goblin turned and stared at Elizabeth. "You must go!"

Elizabeth didn't move. She held Jessica's hand tighter.

The goblin growled. "Elizabeth must go!"

Slowly Jessica smiled. She slipped her hand out of Elizabeth's and pushed the Halloween goblin away. She wasn't scared anymore.

"Charlie Cashman," Jessica said, "why don't you grow up?"

Giggling came from behind the coffin.

Jessica thought back to the kissing couple she had seen earlier. "I know why you keep bugging me," she told the goblin. "You *like* me. You have a crush on me, don't you?"

The goblin's mouth snapped shut. He dropped his hands.

"Do you want a kiss?" Jessica asked him, grinning.

"Gross!" the goblin yelled. His voice sounded just like Charlie's.

Jessica pursed her lips. "Kissy, kissy."

The goblin turned and ran out through the door.

"Look who's scared now!" Jessica called after him.

Elizabeth giggled.

Jessica felt happy. She knew Charlie would never bother her again. "Come on," she told Elizabeth. "I hope the rest of the haunted house is scarier than that dumb goblin."

Todd popped out from inside the coffin. Kisho and Jerry came around from behind the coffin.

"Hey, Elizabeth," Kisho yelled. "Wait for us!"

Three days later, Jessica and Elizabeth came home from trick-or-treating. They found their parents in the den, looking at an atlas.

"Hi, Mom! Hi, Dad!" Jessica called.

She was dressed as a mermaid.

"We're back," Elizabeth added. She was dressed as the Penguin from the Batman comics.

"Did you have a good time?" Mrs. Wakefield asked.

"Great," Elizabeth said. She held up a shopping bag full of candy and chocolate.

"Did you get any good stuff?" Mr. Wakefield asked.

Jessica nodded. "I saved some candy corn for you."

Mr. Wakefield smiled. "Yum. My favorite."

Just then the front door banged shut.

"I bet that's a ghost," Jessica said.

A figure appeared in the doorway. It was wearing a long sheet that glowed in the dark. "Boo!"

"Hi, Steven," Elizabeth said.

Mr. Wakefield turned to Mrs. Wakefield. "Everyone's here. Maybe we should tell them."

"Tell us what?" Jessica asked immediately.

Elizabeth put her bag down and sat next to her mother. "I'm ready!"

"Yeah," Steven said. "What's up?"

"It has to do with Thanksgiving weekend," Mrs. Wakefield said.

"We have special plans," Mr. Wakefield announced. "We're going to leave right after our Thanksgiving dinner and spend the rest of the long weekend on an Indian reservation."

Jessica and Elizabeth exchanged excited looks.

"Awesome!" Steven said.

"Indians," Elizabeth said dreamily. "I wonder what they'll be like."

*Will the twins be surprised by the Native Americans they meet? Find out in Sweet Valley Kids #44, **THE TWINS' BIG POW-WOW.***

☎

1 (800) I LUV BKS!

If you'd like to hear more about your
favorite young adult novels and writers . . .
OR
If you'd like to tell us what you thought
of this book or other books
you've recently read . . .

CALL US at 1(800) I LUV BKS
[1(800) 458-8257]

You'll hear a new message about books and
other interesting subjects each month.

**The call is free to you, but please get
your parents' permission first.**